NOBODY KNOWS

NOBODY KNOWS

by
Shelley Tanaka

From the film by
Hirokazu Kore-eda

Groundwood Books / House of Anansi Press
Toronto   Berkeley

Groundwood Books / House of Anansi Press
110 Spadina Avenue, Suite 801, Toronto, Ontario M5V 2K4
or c/o Publishers Group West
1700 Fourth Street, Berkeley, CA 94710

Special thanks to Miyuki Fukuma (TV Man Union, Inc.)

We acknowledge for their financial support of our publishing program the Canada
Council for the Arts, the Government of Canada through the Canada Book Fund (CBF)
and the Ontario Arts Council.

Canada Council   Conseil des Arts
for the Arts   du Canada

ONTARIO ARTS COUNCIL
CONSEIL DES ARTS DE L'ONTARIO

Library and Archives Canada Cataloguing in Publication
Tanaka, Shelley
Nobody knows / Shelley Tanaka ; from the film by Hirokazu
Kore-eda.
ISBN 978-1-55498-140-3 (bound).—ISBN 978-1-55498-118-2 (pbk.)
I. Title.
PS8589.A775N62 2012   jC813'.54   C2012-902705-7

Cover photograph copyright © Hirokazu Kore-eda
Photos pages 87, 110 and 120 copyright © Kawauchi Rinko
All other photos copyright © Hirokazu Kore-eda
Design by Michael Solomon

Groundwood Books is committed to protecting our natural environment.
As part of our efforts, the interior of this book is printed on paper that contains 100%
post-consumer recycled fibers, is acid-free and is processed chlorine-free.
Printed and bound in Canada

Although this story was inspired by actual events that took place in Tokyo, the details and characters portrayed in this novel are entirely fictional.

AUTUMN

AKIRA TRIED to look tall as his mother rang the bell of the landlord's apartment. His fists felt like knots as they waited for someone to open the door. He could hear a sharp little bark inside and the sound of shuffling slippers.

The man was old and a bit bent over. His sweater was baggy and blue. Just behind him stood his wife. She was slim and dressed up, her fingers polished, her arms lined with bracelets. She held a fat little black-and-white dog that stared out at Akira with bulging black eyes.

Akira tried not to fidget as his mother and their new landlords bowed and were polite.

"We're the Fukushimas," his mother said. She bowed again and held out the present they had brought, a box of tea. "We've just moved into 203. This is just a small thing, a token gift."

"Thank you for going to the trouble," the landlord said, taking the box. He tried to hand it to his wife, but her arms were too full of dog. "It's very nice to meet you."

"My husband is…abroad, you see. So really it's just the two of us. Me and my son." Akira's mother nudged him to say something.

He bowed. "Akira Fukushima."

The dog made a sound in its throat, quite deep for such a little dog.

The landlord stared at Akira and squinted. "Are you in junior high?"

"I'm in…sixth grade."

"You're quite big." The man nodded. "Once you get to this age it's fine, but other tenants tend to complain about little ones. That's why we don't allow children."

"Oh, he's very mature," Akira's mother said quickly. "He'll be no trouble. Fortunately, he takes after his father." She giggled and smiled. "And he's a very good student."

The conversation took forever to wind down, with more bows and smiles and thank-yous. But the landlords shut the door at last, and Akira and his mother went to meet the moving truck. It was just a small truck, but it was filled with boxes and furniture.

Two large suitcases had been the last to go in. One was bright pink, the kind with a hard case. The other was brown and a bit smaller.

"We'll take care of the cases," Akira told the moving men, and he and his mother carefully lifted them out of the truck. They were heavy, and it was hard to get them up the narrow stairs. His mother wasn't very strong. He cringed every time the case bumped against the wall.

"Did you see how young his wife is?" his mother whispered as they finally rolled the cases down the hall and into the apartment. "Apparently he just re-married. I'll bet his first wife died."

But Akira was barely listening, his hand on the top of the suitcase, rolling it gently into the apartment.

At last they were able to close the door on the movers. And just in time, too. The pink suitcase was starting to wobble back and forth.

"We're coming, Shigeru!" Mother said, and they rushed over and carefully lowered the suitcase onto its side. "Just hold on."

She clicked the buckles and opened the lid, and out popped eight-year-old Shigeru with a big grin.

"Here's our noisy boy! Was it hot in there?"

"Way hot." He scrubbed his head with his fists and blinked in the bright light.

Akira was already unzipping the brown suitcase. This one contained four-year-old Yuki, curled up like a flower bud and clutching a small stuffed pink rabbit. But her eyes were open, and she was smiling, one of her pigtails plastered to her hot cheek.

Akira stopped holding his breath. He helped Yuki out of the suitcase.

"Were you hot, too?" Mother gave Yuki a big hug, and the little girl nodded. "You did a great job!"

"Where are we?" Yuki asked, looking around at the room crowded with boxes.

"This is our new home. We're on the second floor. Apartment 203." Mother looked up to see Shigeru bouncing out onto the balcony. "Shige! Get back inside. Akira, bring him in. If they see you we'll have to move all over again. Look, come here and you can start unpacking your toys."

Akira steered his little brother back into the room and slid the balcony door closed.

"Can I get Kyoko now?" he asked.

"Yes, but be careful. You know the way to the station?"

"I know it."

He ran almost the whole way, but his sister was still waiting, sitting alone on the curb by the bicycle racks.

"You're late," she said, as she stood up. She was only ten, but she was almost as tall as he was.

"I'm sorry."

"What's it like, the apartment? Is it big?"

"Pretty big."

"What about a washing machine?"

"On the balcony."

"On the balcony, huh?"

When they arrived back at the apartment building, Kyoko waited downstairs while Akira checked to make sure the hallway was clear and it was safe for her to come up.

With the five of them in it, the apartment didn't seem that big at all. There was one main room with a kitchen at one end and a table and chairs. At the other end were sliding doors to the balcony and space for sleeping on the floor. A large television stood in the corner. There was also a small back room for chests of drawers and Mother's dressing table, and a bathroom.

But none of that mattered to Akira. It just felt so good to be together, arguing over whether to put carrots in the soup, fighting over the big chopsticks and who got the most noodles.

They sat around the little table. There were only four real chairs, but Shige pulled over a tippy yellow folding stool for himself and knelt on it to eat. Mother looked happy, and it was wonderful to see her laughing and joking with them all.

But finally she tapped her chopsticks on the table to get everyone's attention, and her voice became serious.

"Now that we have moved into a new home," she said, "I'm going to explain the rules to you one more time. You must promise to obey them, okay?"

They nodded. They all knew how important this was.

"First of all, no loud noises or yelling."

"Shige, too?"

"Especially Shige. Next, no going outside, not even onto the balcony. Can you do that? Can you promise?"

"How will Kyoko wash the clothes?" Yuki asked.

"Kyoko will sneak out quietly to do the laundry. But, Shigeru and Yuki, you two must stay inside. Akira, you'll be in charge. And study a lot. Do you understand?"

Yuki looked at the others and nodded her head up and down for all of them.

"What about you, my little Shige monster?" Mother said. "You're the one who has to promise the hardest. Absolutely no going outside. Can you do that?"

Shige scrunched up his nose and made his monster face, but he bobbed his chin up and down and slurped his noodles.

Mother looked at him sternly. "Remember the last place? We had to leave because you threw such tantrums. So now that we have this nice new home, you have to promise."

They all looked hard at Shige.

"What if I have to laugh?" he asked finally.

"We'll make you eat green peppers and carrots!"

"No, no! Not peppers!" Shige shook his head back and forth. A huge grin crossed his face.

"We'll give Shige the green pepper punishment!" said Mother. "And if that doesn't work, the next time you feel a tantrum coming on, it's...back into the suitcase. Just put him in the suitcase if he gets noisy, okay?"

"Great idea." Akira nodded with the others, and he grinned, too.

They all slept together that night, side by side on the tatami mats. It was cozy in their nest of pillows and quilts.

"Mother?" It was Kyoko, lying on her stomach.

"Hmmm?"

"These tatami mats smell good."

"They do? What do they smell like?"

"Like leaves in nature."

"It's because the tatami are new. They're still green. They'll give you sweet dreams."

Autumn

Akira turned his head and took a deep breath. The mats did smell good. He closed his eyes, listening to the breathing of his family all around him.

It was going to be okay here. A fresh start for all of them. He just knew it.

Akira brushed his teeth and watched his mother putting on her makeup the next morning. She looked nice, with her long thick hair framing her face. She was wearing her favorite blouse, a soft and ruffly black top with white flowers. It made her look very pretty, very slim and young.

"Will you be late getting home tonight?" he asked.

"Late?" She leaned closely into the mirror. She took her makeup very seriously, carefully brushing on lip gloss and mascara with mysterious little wands. Her dressing table was covered with tiny pots and perfume bottles.

She thought for a moment. "Let's see. What's today? Oh, I guess so. Maybe. Maybe I'll be late."

"Do you want dinner?" he asked. If she was going to be late, he wouldn't bother cooking anything. Maybe just noodles for the four of them.

"Dinner? What is for dinner tonight?"

"Maybe curry."

"Curry? Yes, I want curry! Save me some, please." And then she was off, tapping down the hall in her high heels even before the door had clicked shut behind her.

"Hey, has Mom gone already?" Kyoko called sleepily from the floor.

"She just left."

Kyoko jumped up and ran to the window. But their mother was already on the bridge over the canal. She was practically running. Maybe she was late.

There was lots to do in the apartment. Akira put away the dishes and kitchen things. He folded up the empty boxes and put them out in the hall. Yuki and Kyoko slowly unpacked their books and toys. Kyoko found a spot for her favorite treasure, a shiny red toy piano.

But even after they had finished unpacking the most important things, the walls of the apartment were still lined with boxes and bags. It almost looked as though they were about to move all over again.

Shige mostly got in the way, raiding the fridge for snacks and drinks, leaving his robot collection scattered over every surface. They sent him to sit in his suitcase more than once. He didn't mind. In the end he turned it into a kind of throne and slumped in front of the TV, clicking the remote madly and flicking from show to show.

In the afternoon, Akira went out to shop and explore. Their new apartment was in a nice neighborhood beside the canal, close to a busy shopping street. There was a *konbini* convenience store, a hardware store, a video arcade, everything.

He ran through his list in his head, trying to remember the things he needed to buy. He'd promised Yuki a box of her favorite Apollo chocolates — little strawberry-flavored candies shaped like tiny pink-and-brown spaceships. Yuki could play with them for hours, lining them up, counting them, eating them one at a time. Couldn't forget those.

He shopped carefully. He knew they had to watch how they spent their money. It cost a lot to feed a family of five. He sniffed the persimmons, squeezed the pears, checked the potatoes for soft spots. He had to go to three places before he found Yuki's candies in the convenience store closest to their place.

It was almost dark by the time he got home. Kyoko had done a laundry, and she helped him get dinner ready. The kitchen was tiny, but they managed. Kyoko made the rice. He washed the potatoes, chopped the vegetables. The apartment filled with a good spicy smell. Curry was one of his specialties.

He knew that not many twelve-year-olds shopped and cooked for their families every night. Most boys his age were busy with school and sports. But this was the way it had to be if they were all going to stay together...

"Are you okay?" Kyoko asked when she saw him wiping his eyes.

He nodded. It was only tears from chopping the onions.

Shige poked his head over the counter.

"Are there carrots?"

"Yes."

"None for me."

"No, you have to eat them," Akira said. He knew it wouldn't make any difference. Shige only ate vegetables when he was very, very hungry.

It was late by the time Mother came home. The dishes had been washed, the carrots scraped into the garbage. Kyoko was in her pajamas, hanging wet socks and underwear from the little plastic laundry hanger that dangled from the curtain rod. Akira had made sure the little ones had had their baths and brushed their teeth. They were already asleep. Now he was trying to do some schoolwork.

"She's home!" Kyoko whispered from the window. She ran to the door and listened for the sound of footsteps out in the hallway, her hand on the door handle. She flung the door open just as their mother reached the apartment.

"I'm back!" Mother called out, pulling off her shoes. "Brrr, it's so cold out there. Nice and warm in here, though. Kyoko, why aren't you in bed?"

"I was hanging the laundry." She turned on the stove to warm up the curry.

"What a good girl." Mother patted her cheek and smiled. "Thank you. And what do we have here?" She sniffed the pot. "Mmmm, smells good. Can I have some?"

She threw her bag and shawl on the little yellow stool. Then she sat down and leaned over Akira's notebook.

"Did I get this right?" he asked. He knew he could look up the answers in the back of the book, but he liked it when she helped him. "I hate math."

"Come on, six times six is…" She poked him with the pencil and it tickled. "Hurry up, you can— "

But her phone was ringing, and right away she was poking around in her bag trying to find her cell phone. She had a ridiculous pink pompom attached to it, but she never seemed to be able to find it anyway.

"Hello? I can hardly hear you…" She pushed away from the table just as Kyoko was placing her bowl of curry in front of her.

Akira listened as his mother moved into the other room, trying to hear the person on the other end of the line.

"What? Where did you say you were? It's so noisy there… What, karaoke? No, I can't… it's too late. What? Who else is there? Really? What a shame…"

Nobody Knows

She closed the door behind her. Akira stared down at his notebook.

Suddenly the numbers looked all crooked on the page, like some strange language.

JUST A LITTLE sliver of light was shining through the drapes when Akira opened his eyes the next morning. He listened to the others around him, their breathing soft and steady. It was snug being together like this, with Shige beside him and the girls on the other side of their mother.

His mother looked very young when she slept. Some people said she and Kyoko and Yuki practically looked like sisters. When they did, she would giggle, and her cheeks would turn pink with happiness.

He watched her now. Her eyes were closed, the back of her hand resting on her forehead. Without any makeup, her face looked so smooth and peaceful and...

At first he thought it was a trick of the light, but it wasn't. It was a tear sliding down his mother's face.

She was crying. They were finally all together again, in their own place, and she was crying.

She sighed then, and sat up. She rubbed her eyes with her fists like a little kid. Then she stretched her arms and looked at each of her children in turn.

But by the time she turned to Akira, his eyes were closed.

He woke up again an hour later to the sound of Shige turning on the television. Akira rolled up the futon and got dressed. His mother and the girls were sitting at the little dressing table doing girl stuff. Mother was putting Yuki's hair in pigtails with her favorite monkey barrettes. She put hairclips in her bunny's ears, too. Kyoko played with Mother's makeup, opening all the fancy little jars, sniffing each one.

Kyoko suddenly stared at her mother in the mirror.

"Mother?"

"Hmm?" Mother started to brush Kyoko's hair now, making the part straight, smoothing it behind her ears.

"I want to go to school."

Mother stopped brushing. She frowned.

"School?" She started brushing again, a little

more roughly. "You wouldn't have any fun at school. Besides, when you don't have a daddy, the other kids bully you. You don't need to go to school."

Akira saw his sister's face fall. He knew how desperate Kyoko was to go to school. She couldn't even read properly yet, though he tried to teach her what he knew. She wanted to learn how to play the piano. She wanted a best friend.

Well, she couldn't have what she wanted. None of them could. It was just too bad.

Mother came out to the balcony a little later when he was airing out the bedding. The sun shone warm on their faces.

His mother leaned her chin on the railing. She buried her face in the quilt.

"Smells good, huh?" he said.

"Stinks of sunlight." She squinted into the sun. "What a beautiful day." She sighed. She had a dreamy, faraway look in her eyes.

That was never a good sign…

"I have to tell you something, Akira."

"What?" He didn't look at her.

"Your mother is…in love."

"Again?"

She looked at him and pushed out her lower lip.

"No, not *again*. This is serious. This guy is really sweet. He cares about me, he looks out for me. So this time... if he really promises... to marry me, then we can all live in a big house and you can all go to school and Kyoko can have a real piano and... " She turned and looked him right in the eye. "Just hang on a little longer, okay? I really think this is it this time. Just a little longer..."

He nodded. Then he buried his face in the quilt and breathed in the stink of sunshine.

It was after midnight, and their mother still hadn't come home. She had been coming back later and later all week.

Akira sat at the table and watched his brother and sisters sleep. Even Kyoko had finally got tired of waiting up. Shige slept with his mouth open, his foot twitching from time to time. Kyoko lay on her stomach, her hand on Mother's pillow. Yuki snuggled into her sister, her stuffed bunny clutched in her fist.

Akira shook his head to try to keep himself awake. He was trying to do some schoolwork, but the numbers swam in front of his eyes. It was hard learning just from a book, with no teacher.

He heard a car stop in the quiet street outside. He tiptoed to the window and peered out from behind the curtain. His mother was waving at a taxi as it drove off. Several white plastic bags dangled from her arms. She kept waving and smiling until the cab turned the corner at the end of the street.

Akira went back to the table and laid his head on his arms. He pretended to sleep, even when he heard her fumbling with the door handle.

"I'm home!" she cried as she burst into the apartment. She plopped her bags on the table and mussed up his hair.

"I'm home!" she said again. She plopped down on the futon and tickled Kyoko, meowing into her ear like a pussycat. "Were you asleep? Come on, guys. I brought sushi. It's a present. Wake up!"

Akira looked at his mother. She was wound up, her eyes bright.

He sighed and put on the kettle. He began to pull dishes out of the cupboard.

Kyoko sat up, rubbing her eyes.

"Now?" she asked.

"It's a sushi present!" Mother said. "Oh, were you sleeping? Are you mad? Come on, Yuki. Over here." Yuki crawled over and cuddled into her mother's side.

Shige ran over to the table and started to rummage through the boxes of sushi.

Kyoko stomped to the sink and poured a glass of water.

"She stinks of booze," she muttered to Akira. She took the water and handed it to her mother.

"Here, Mom. Drink this."

"Thank you, sweetie." Her mother looked up at her with big eyes. Her grin was sloppy and lopsided. Akira hated when she got like this, all silly and stupid.

"Come on, sit beside me. I'm sorry I woke you. It's just that your mommy had a pretty good time to-night." She leaned her head against the wall and put her arms around Yuki and Kyoko. She looked over at the boys. Akira was getting out tea cups.

"Look at Akira, getting so grown-up," she said, her voice all dreamy. "He's starting to look just like his father. He's got his father's eyes exactly." She turned to Yuki. "Your brother's father used to work at Haneda. You know what Haneda is, Yuki? It's a place with lots of planes."

Yuki smiled and nodded happily. She loved air-planes.

"You remember, Akira? Taking the train to Haneda Airport to see your father?"

"Yeah." She was confusing his father with Shige's dad, but he couldn't be bothered to correct her. She was too drunk, anyway.

"And, Kyoko, your father was a…music producer. I wanted to be a singer. Nearly made it, too. I was going to cut a record but the deal…well, it fell through at the last minute…" She sighed and patted Kyoko's hand. "I know! Let's give Kyoko a nice manicure. Would you like that?"

Kyoko smiled and nodded. Her mother reached for her purse and pulled out a bottle of bright red nail polish. She held Kyoko's hand and started to paint her nails with shaky strokes.

"Oops! I'm using too much," she giggled. The brush dripped polish on the quilt, but she didn't notice. She finished Kyoko's left hand and then suddenly seemed to lose interest. Her head slumped back against the pillows.

"Yes, I was going to be a singer," she muttered, her eyelids closing. "But the deal fell through…"

Akira reached behind him and turned off the kettle. He began to put away the tea cups.

Shige sat at the table munching on sushi, right out of the box. His grin was huge.

It was salmon. His favorite.

Akira was surprised to see that his mother had already left for work when he woke up the next morning. He left the curtains closed so that the others could sleep. They had all been up late and besides, there was nothing to get up for, really. No place they had to be.

He went to the fridge and poured himself a glass of milk. It took a while before he noticed the note on the table. He had to hold it up to read in the dim light:

Dear Akira:
Your mother is going away for a little while.
Please look after Kyoko, Shigeru and Yuki.

Under the note was an envelope full of money. Akira fanned out the 10,000 yen notes.

It looked like a lot. It looked like it was meant to last a long time.

He didn't know what to tell the others, so he didn't say anything at first.

Finally, when Shige and Yuki were busy playing inside, he went out to the balcony where Kyoko was doing the laundry. She was admiring the bright red nails on her left hand, rubbing off little flecks of polish with her finger to try to tidy up the messy manicure. Kyoko had slender fingers like their mother. Her red fingertips sparkled like jewels in the sunlight.

"I'm going shopping," Akira said to his sister.

"Okay."

"Oh, and also," he said quickly, "Mother won't be coming back for a while."

"Why not?"

"Something to do with work, I think. Anyway, I'm off." And he slipped back into the apartment and slid the glass door closed behind him.

The neighborhood convenience store really had everything they needed. Groceries, toys, a magazine rack, sushi and food for takeout. Even socks and umbrellas.

Nobody Knows

Akira wandered around slowly, taking his time. He stopped at the shelf of action figures. They even had Jetfire, his favorite. As soon as there was enough money, that's the one he would buy first.

He paid for his things and stopped to check out the comics. Lots of kids hung around the magazine rack. The clerks didn't seem to mind.

But he knew the others would be waiting, so after a while he picked up his bags and walked out of the store.

He was only half a block down the street when he felt a sharp yank on his sweatshirt.

It was the manager of the convenience store.

"Come with me," the man said. His hand on Akira's shoulder felt heavy as he turned him around. "To my office."

In the office at the back of the store, he reached into Akira's bag and pulled out three boxes of action figures. He lined them up on his desk like a little army and glared at Akira.

"Have you done this before?" he said gruffly.

"No."

"Your first time?"

"I didn't take anything." Akira didn't know how the boxes had got in his bag, but he knew the less he said, the better.

"Then what's all this?" The man looked angry now. "What's your name?"

"Akira Fukushima."

The manager wrote it down. "Your school?"

Akira said nothing. He pressed his fists to his sides.

"Your father's name?" the man pressed.

"I don't have a father."

"No father? Your mother, then?"

"She's gone away to work for a while."

"Where did she go? If you won't tell me, I'll have to call the police."

Akira felt the sweat start to run down between his shoulder blades. He knew what that meant. More and more questions, and then social services would get involved. The last time that happened the four of them had been separated for a long time, and his mother nearly went crazy.

There was a small knock at the door. It was one of the store clerks. A girl with a nice smile. She bowed and took a nervous step into the room.

"What is it?" the manager shouted.

She bowed again.

"Sir, I don't think this boy stole those things. I think other boys reading comics put them in his bag."

"You're saying it wasn't him?"

"No, I don't think so."

The man sighed and rubbed his forehead. "Why on earth didn't you speak up before?"

"I'm sorry."

"Don't I'm sorry me." He reached down, handed Akira his bag and steered him to the front of the store. "Okay, no harm done. This can just stay between us, all right? Here, take some meat buns as a little bonus." He turned to the clerk. "Hurry up, give him some."

Akira waited as the clerk filled a small bag.

"Thank you. Thank you very much," he said as he took the buns. He nodded at her with relief, but when he left the store, his hands were still shaking.

AKIRA HAD told his mother he hated math, but now he seemed to be doing it all the time. Not in a workbook, though. Instead he was always adding and subtracting, trying to figure out how much money they had left, how much he could spend on food after the electricity and rent and other bills were paid.

Some days he felt like a living math problem: *Akira spent 740 yen at the supermarket. He had 6,500 yen left in his wallet. How many yen did Akira have in his wallet to begin with?*

The worst thing was not knowing how long it would be until she came back.

Finally, when they were down to the last 10,000 yen, he decided he had to do something.

It took many stops and transfers on the subway, but it wasn't that hard to find Yuki's father at the taxi garage on the other side of the city. Most of the cars were out on duty. Akira found the man sleeping in his cab, snoring in the passenger seat, his mouth open, his uniform stretched tight across his fat belly. He didn't even move when Akira knocked on the window, so Akira just sat on a nearby stack of tires and waited.

The guy had to wake up some time.

When he did, he barely looked at Akira before he headed inside to use the toilet. But Akira just waited, and soon he returned, and he couldn't ignore him any longer.

They sat together in the cab. The man fiddled around with his phone for a while, then gave a big sigh.

"How's your mother?"

Akira didn't waste any time. "She hasn't been home in a month."

"Are you kidding?" The man wouldn't look at him. "How old are you, Akira?"

"Twelve."

"And Yuki? Does she take after me?"

What a stupid question. This guy had never even lived with them. His eyes were like little slits in his chubby face. It was hard to believe he was Yuki's father.

"Yes, she does."

The man shoved a stick of gum in his mouth. He didn't offer any to Akira.

Akira knew then that it was hopeless. This guy was nothing but a jerk.

He left the man staring at his phone and walked back to the subway. He checked the address in his pocket and studied the subway map for a long time.

At the other end of the train line the pachinko parlor was crowded, smoky and noisy. Kids weren't normally allowed in here, but nobody gave Akira a second look

as he walked up and down the rows, past one customer after another. They were all feeding coins into
these machines so they could bang some levers to try
to stop a stupid little ball from dropping down into a
trough.

Why not play video games instead, Akira wondered. More challenging. More fun.

He found his own father down a crowded aisle,
emptying cash out of one of the machines. When he
saw Akira he quickly waved him away and signaled
that he would meet him outside.

Akira waited in the parking lot for his father to
finish his shift. It began to rain. He practiced in his
head what he would say. He wasn't going to go away
empty-handed this time.

His father came out in a rush and headed straight
for the vending machine.

"Akira! Shit, man, I'm ten yen short. Lend me ten
yen."

"Ten yen?" He couldn't believe his father was asking him for money, but he pulled out his wallet.

"Come on, what's the big deal? And where did you
get that ridiculous wallet?"

"It's Mother's. Her old one."

"Whose?" He tossed a drink to Akira and they leaned against the wall of the parking lot watching the cold rain.

"My mother." His father was almost as bad as Yuki's dad. But Akira was not going to be put off this time.

"You moved, right?" his father said. "Is the new place big? Got any pubic hair yet?"

"What? No..."

"Liar. I got mine in fifth grade."

Akira looked at the man sideways. Maybe this was the kind of thing sons and fathers talked about, but how would he know?

"No way," he said.

"It's the truth, man."

They were quiet for a minute. His drink can was almost empty. He had to say something.

"It's just... since Mother's been gone, well, there's no money."

"Are you kidding? Listen, I don't have any. How much have you got left?"

"About ten thousand yen."

"That's not bad. Hey, I'm in a hell of a jam myself. My girlfriend maxed out my credit cards. I'm in credit card hell, man. That's why I'm working my ass off, trying to pay it down."

Akira said nothing. Just stood there and stared right at him.

"Okay," his father said finally. He reached into his pocket and handed Akira a folded bill. "This is all I've got on me. Man, this is it, though. The last time."

"Thank you."

"Sure." He reached out and patted Akira's head, almost like a real dad. "Oh, and just so you know. Yuki's not my kid. Every time I did it with your mom, I used a condom." He chucked his empty drink can into the air and it landed neatly in the garbage. Then he waved once before he disappeared back inside.

Akira looked at the money in his hand. Five thousand yen. He tucked it deep in his pocket. He eyed the trash can, took aim, pulled his arm back and pitched. The can hit the wall and clattered down the alley.

"I'm useless," he muttered, as he trotted over to pick it up and lob it into the garbage. He shivered and pulled up the collar of his jacket before he headed out into the rain.

"Man, it's cold."

It was early November when she burst into the apartment like a swarm of pigeons, all cold air and hurry and rustling packages.

"I'm home!" she cried, like she was just coming home for dinner after a day at work. "How have you guys been?"

Akira held the door stiffly while she squeezed in with her shopping bags. The little ones leaped up to greet her. Kyoko slowly closed the picture book she had been looking at with Yuki. She didn't get up.

"See? I'm home," Mother cried again. "Look, I brought presents. This one's for Yuki. And for Shige. See, Akira, I'm home." She turned to Akira and reached out, but he pulled back before she could touch him.

"It's been a while, Akira," she said. He wouldn't look her in the eye.

She wanted them all to open their gifts right away, and even Kyoko and Akira joined in. The little ones were so happy. Yuki put on her new backpack. It was shaped like a teddy bear.

"See?" said Mother. "You can put your things in it, and carry it on your back."

Akira and Kyoko just looked at each other. What would Yuki do with a backpack? She wasn't even allowed to leave the apartment.

Later, Mother cut the boys' hair, and it was almost like she'd never been gone. The apartment smelled different with her at home, all flowery with perfume and the smell of fresh air.

Yuki stood pressed against her mother's side as she snipped and combed.

"What's with that face?" Mother said when she saw Shige staring in the mirror and rubbing his hands over his brush cut. "It looks cute. I mean it. Don't you think your brothers look better with short hair, Yuki? Which do you like, short or long?"

"Long."

"What about you, Kyoko?" But Kyoko was hanging the laundry. She didn't answer.

"Well, too bad. I'm cutting it anyway. Okay, Akira?"

He kept quiet. She was cutting it too short, but what could he say?

In the mirror he saw Kyoko wander over to Mother's purse. She reached into the bag and took out the bottle of red nail polish. She unscrewed the top and sniffed. The rich sharp smell of polish filled the room.

Suddenly the bottle slipped out of her hand. Kyoko gasped and looked down at the shiny blood-red puddle on the wood floor.

"Hey, what are you doing?" Her mother rushed over, frowning. "Don't touch my things!" She grabbed some tissues and started mopping up the stain, making even more of a mess. "Look what you've done! It's your fault. Now it won't come out—"

"Where were you, Mother?" Kyoko asked. Her voice was flat, and a little bit hard.

Akira held his breath.

"What? I told you. I was working."

"For a whole month?"

"I was in Osaka. It was just too far." She kept

wiping the nail polish. She was using too many tissues.

Couldn't she see she was making it worse?

"I told you not to touch my things." And she gathered up the tissues and stomped away.

Kyoko was still holding the lid of the bottle with the little brush. Akira saw her look down at the stain the polish had left on the floor.

Then she painted a stripe of red on her finger and stared at it for a long time.

IT WAS YUKI who noticed first, a few hours later. Akira and Shige were playing with Shige's new remote-controlled robots. Kyoko was tapping out a tune on her little piano.

It was almost as if they had all forgotten their mother was back.

But Yuki had been watching.

"What are you doing?" she asked. Mother was pulling clothes out of the closet, folding them and putting them in a bag.

"What? Oh, well, you see, your mother has to go out, so I'm getting ready."

Akira stood up. She hadn't even been back for a day.

"You're going already?" Shige said.

"Your mother is…busy today. But don't worry. I'll be back for Christmas."

Akira walked her to the station. She wanted him to wear the new scarf she had brought him, so he did. It was orange and white. It looked like a girl's scarf.

"Only five thousand yen?" she said, when he told her about seeing his father. "He could have given you a little more. I mean, you're just kids and you're in a jam. But, hey, pachinko parlors and taxis don't draw many customers in such hard times. But you go back to him if you need to." She shivered, clutched her coat to her neck and kept walking. "It's so cold. So windy."

Akira stopped. He stared at her back. He had to say something.

"Did you tell that man you're seeing about us?"

His mother stopped. He could see her shoulders freeze, then heave in a big sigh. She was annoyed.

"I told you, I'll tell him when the time is right…" And she kept walking, faster now.

They went to a Mister Donut near the station. She bought him a donut and they sat across from each other while she watched him eat. He noticed she had dark circles under her eyes. She wasn't wearing as much makeup as usual.

The donut was very sweet. He chewed, and the

dough formed into a sticky ball at the back of his throat.

"You've got sugar on your lip," she teased, and she reached over to brush it off. Akira jerked his head away.

"God, you're so irritating," she said. He knew she was trying to have a nice time before she said good-bye.

He was fed up with her, but she was his mother. She was all they had.

"Listen," he said finally. "We keep asking you. When will you let us go to school?"

She rolled her eyes. "What's with this school business? What's the matter with you? Who needs to go to school, anyway? There are lots of famous people who have never been to school."

"Like who?"

She pouted, poked out her bottom lip the way Yuki did when she was cross.

"How should I know? But there are lots of — "

"You're being so selfish, Mother." There, he'd said it.

"How can you say that?" She was whining now.

"You want to know who's selfish? Your father, that's who. He's the one who's selfish, up and disappearing like that. What is this? I'm not allowed to be happy? What is this?" She crossed her arms and slumped back in her chair. She wouldn't look at him.

The silence stretched between them.

"I know," she said suddenly. He looked up. "I know someone famous. Prime Minister Tanaka. Ever heard of him?"

"Never." What was she talking about?

"You're too young. Okay, then, how about ... Antonio Inoki."

A smile twitched at the corners of his mouth. The wrestler? What did he have to do with anything? His mother was just so crazy...

"I'll bet Inoki never went to school," she said. "I'm not sure, but..."

"Sure he did." But Akira broke into a grin anyway.

"Man, you're such a drag," she said. "Go on, finish your donut."

At the station she was in a hurry to get away, he could tell.

"I'll send you more money," she said. "Soon."

"You'll come home for Christmas?" he asked. She reached over to muss up his hair, and this time he let her.

"Sure, I'll come home. Soon. Take care of them, okay?"

And he lost sight of her quickly as she pushed through the turnstile with her bags and disappeared into the crowd.

WINTER

NOVEMBER PASSED, and the weather grew colder. Still, the four of them managed. She sent more money, and even Shige got used to their indoor life. He started talking to himself. He would set up a board game and play against himself, muttering away in some made-up language. He would make his move and then jump up and switch to the other side of the board.

Yuki drew lots of pictures — mostly pictures of a smiling woman with big black eyes and red lips and long wavy hair. Kyoko taped the drawings to the refrigerator or the wall, until the smiling woman seemed to look at them from every side of the apartment.

As Christmas drew closer, the two girls decorated the apartment with little pieces of foil saved from soup lids, stickers from groceries and colored pictures cut out of flyers.

"Santa will come, won't he?" said Yuki at dinner one evening. They were sitting around the table. Shige had pulled the tippy yellow folding stool over for himself. Their mother's chair was empty. Yuki didn't like anyone else to sit there.

In front of each of them sat a container of instant noodles, fresh from the microwave. Now they had to wait three minutes. Shige put the kitchen timer on the table and tapped his foot, making little drum sounds. The others laughed as he kept lifting the lid with the tip of his chopstick, as if that would make the noodles ready faster.

The helpings were large, but Kyoko had made rice, too. Later Shige would add spoonfuls to his leftover broth. He was always hungry these days, even after the others were full.

"You think Santa is real?" Akira said, grinning at Kyoko.

"He is. I know it," Shige said, shaking the clock. "One more minute!"

"Real like UFOs?" Akira asked.

"Nope."

"Nope," agreed Yuki.

"If Martians are real, so are UFOs," Akira said.

Yuki looked at Shige. But her brother was watching the timer.

It dinged.

"Ready!" he cried. And he peeled the top off his noodles and licked the lid.

"*Itadakimasu*," said Yuki. "Thanks for the food."

"Yes, *itadakimasu*. Let's eat!" And they all dug in.

SHE SAID SHE would be home for Christmas, but she didn't come. On Christmas Eve, Akira went out. The shopping street was decorated with fat plastic Santas and blinking colored lights.

Outside the convenience store, the clerks were dressed in Santa costumes, selling boxes of Christmas cake for two thousand yen. The cakes were decorated with white icing and strawberries. Yuki's favorite.

Akira stood across the street and watched. It was bitterly cold, but he waited anyway, blowing on his fingers to warm them, wishing that his mother had given him gloves instead of the orange-and-white scarf.

Finally, an hour before closing, the clerks reduced the price. Twelve hundred yen. That was good enough.

The streets were almost empty as Akira headed back to the apartment. Everyone had gone home early to be with their families. He balanced the large box carefully as he made his way home in the dark, watching his feet as he walked down the steps beside the canal.

So it was the sound that caught his attention at first. The dull sound of objects plopping into the water.

He stopped and looked up. A girl was standing in the middle of the bridge over the canal. She seemed to be taking books out of her schoolbag and tossing them into the water one at a time.

Why would anyone throw books into the water?

She must have felt him looking at her. She turned. Under the streetlight her face was white, like a ghost's. When she saw Akira staring, she quickly closed her bag and ran past him into the dark.

"SHE DIDN'T COME," Kyoko said. They were washing dishes together. He had used too much detergent, and now it was hard to rinse the dishes properly in the tiny sink.

"It's because of her work," Akira said. "That's why she had to stay away longer."

"It's because I was so mean to her when she was home, isn't it?"

"No. That's not it at all."

But Kyoko just put down her dishtowel and walked away, leaving him with his arms deep in bubbles.

She didn't come home for New Year's Eve, either. She didn't send *otoshidama*, the little white envelopes filled with money that she always gave them, with their names carefully printed on the back.

It made him so mad. Couldn't she at least have done that?

He found the special envelopes in the store, but he knew his handwriting wasn't good enough to write the names. Kyoko would never be fooled.

It was pure luck that he walked past the laundromat. He saw the nice girl clerk from the convenience store through the window, and she was happy to help him. He made her address an envelope for himself, too.

"Mom sent us all New Year's presents!" he announced the next day. "Look!"

They came running, and opened their envelopes one at a time. One thousand yen for Yuki, two thousand for Shige and four thousand for Kyoko.

"Four thousand yen!" Akira said, when he opened his own envelope. "What will you do with yours, Yuki?"

"A doll."

"Shigeru?"

"Rollerblades."

"Kyoko?" He watched her closely. She was putting the envelope in her box of treasures, where he knew she kept every card their mother had ever given her.

He saw her pick up the pile of cards. She paused

for a moment before she slipped the envelope in with the others. Then she looked up, her eyes beaming straight into his.

"I'm saving mine up for a piano. A real one. What about you?"

Akira thought for a moment.

"A glove," he said finally. "A baseball glove."

JANUARY PASSED, and February, too. It was still cold. Sometimes the watery sunshine felt almost like spring. Other times it seemed as though winter would never end.

But still she didn't come home.

And then, one cold evening in March, Yuki said, "I'm going to the station to meet Mommy." She was staring out the window after dinner, her little stuffed bunny propped on the sill.

"But she's not coming home today," Kyoko said.

"She is so. It's my birthday."

It was, too. Akira had forgotten.

"She'll be back next week."

"Really?" Shige asked. "She's coming next week?"

"Yes."

"How do you know?"

"I just do," Akira said.

"No, she's coming today," Yuki said. Her lips made a straight little line and she stared right at him.

Akira looked at Kyoko. Kyoko nodded, and Akira sighed.

It took a long time to get Yuki dressed. Her winter coat was too tight, but Kyoko managed to do it up and wrap her scarf around her neck. She insisted on carrying her new backpack, the one shaped like a teddy. And her bunny, and her chocolates.

Akira reached for her shoes.

"No." Yuki said. "Those ones." She pointed at her bright red slippers with bears on the front. Her heels hung off the back, and the shoes squeaked when she walked.

But today was Yuki's birthday. Today she could have whatever she wanted.

When she was finally ready he peeked out the door into the hallway to make sure the coast was clear. It was, but even though they were careful, luck was not on their side. At the bottom of the stairs they walked right into their landlords.

Akira stopped and bowed. The old man and his

pretty wife smiled when they saw Yuki, all decked out with her teddy-bear backpack, her little face and pigtails practically smothered by her big scarf.

"And where are you off to?" the man asked, bending down to look into her face.

"To the station to meet my mommy," Yuki answered, her small voice muffled.

"I see," said the landlady. She held the fat black-and-white dog in her arms like a baby. It was wrapped in a pink knitted baby blanket. "And what's your name?"

"Yuki."

"And how old are you, Yuki?"

"Five."

"Five years old?" said the landlady.

"She's our cousin," Akira said quickly. "She's just staying overnight." He took Yuki's hand and squeezed it tightly.

"Ah," said the landlord. "I see." And he patted Yuki's head and smiled. "Off you go, then."

"Adorable little girl," said the landlady, kissing the top of her dog's head.

And as they went on their way, Akira's breath made a sudden cloud in the cold air.

He had to walk more slowly than usual with his little sister beside him. She took tiny squeaky steps, partly because her shoes didn't fit, and partly, he realized, because it had been so long since she had been outside. It was almost as though she had forgotten how to walk.

But Yuki didn't care. She couldn't stop looking at the bright storefronts, at all the things displayed in the windows.

"Tomato … daikon … broccoli … squash … carrots … mushrooms," she chanted. "So many … plates … and cups … and …"

At the station they sat on the curb and waited. Akira was freezing, but Yuki didn't seem to mind the cold. She wouldn't leave.

She finished her tiny pink-and-brown candies.

"Oops, only one left," she said sadly, tapping the box. "It's the very last one…"

Akira looked down at his sister, her cheeks rosy, her eyes watching the people streaming past them as they went in and out of the station, her feet squirming with cold in those stupid slippers.

And his heart suddenly felt too full. With anger, or love. He wasn't sure which.

It was very late by the time he convinced Yuki to go home. They walked hand in hand down the middle of the deserted road, her shoes squeaking as she tried to walk along the white line dividing the lanes of the street.

A roar above them made them both look up. The monorail went past like thunder on the track overhead, its lights gleaming.

The noise made the street tremble. Yuki clutched Akira's hand more tightly.

"It's just the train," he told her. "It goes all the way out to Haneda Airport."

"To the planes?" Her eyes were wide.

"Some day I'll take you. We'll get on the train and go and see the airplanes."

"Okay," she said, smiling happily, as though he had just given her the best present ever. "Let's do that."

SPRING

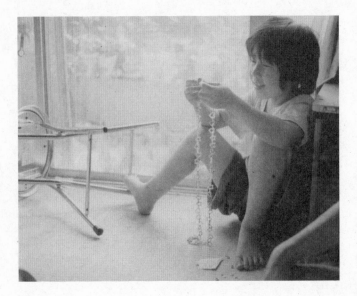

How many weeks passed after that? Akira lost track.
Every day was the same. He would go out to buy food,
to the bank machine to pay the rent or the electricity
or the gas and water bills. It was easy once you knew
how. You just waited for the machine to tell you what
to do. Entered your account number. Punched in the
amount of the transfer.

The other three children stayed in the apartment.
They drew pictures, played with puzzles, watched television. Kyoko tried to make tunes on her little toy piano, but it only had twenty-five keys, and she couldn't do
much. Some days the sun shone right in through the
balcony window, and it was warm enough to open the
sliding door. Over the weeks, Shige edged himself far-
ther out onto the balcony to play, and the others eventually stopped reminding him to stay hidden and inside.

That had just been their mother's rule, anyway.

As the weather grew warmer, Akira was no longer in such a rush to get back to the apartment. He found himself staying out later, reading comics in the convenience store. It made him feel just like all the other kids.

One day he found a shiny rubber ball in the park, and he stopped for a while to play with it. It would have been nice to have a friend to play catch with, but all the other kids were in school. So he just tossed the ball into the air as high as he could, and tried to catch it when it came back down.

If only he had a glove. Or a bat. He tried lobbing the ball in the air and swatting it with a stick, but the rubber ball was too slippery, the stick way too skinny.

Batting practice was hard when you were just one person. Still, it was fun.

The city was coming out of its cold, hard winter. There were more people on the streets, not rushing by quite so fast. Kids came to the video arcade after school.

Then, one day, something was different at the bank machine.

"*Please indicate the amount of your transfer,*" the mechanical voice said. But when Akira punched in the numbers for the electricity bill, nothing happened.

Insufficient funds, said the message on the screen.

"Please indicate the amount of your transfer." He tried again and again, punching in the same numbers, until sweat began to leak down his neck. *"Please indicate the amount of your..."*

He walked away. He didn't want to think about it. About the empty bank account. The shrinking stack of money on the kitchen table.

He wandered home slowly, taking his time. It was nice out, a faint smell of warm earth in the breeze.

He didn't want to go back to the others. Not yet.

Akira slowed outside the arcade. Why shouldn't he go in? He would just watch. No need to spend any money.

That's where he met two guys from the local school. He hung out with them for a bit. They even let him take a turn with Dragon Ball, and then Road-Blasters. He was good at it, too. Didn't have to use the brake, and they were impressed.

Later, on the way home, Akira practically felt like a racing car himself, zooming down the sidewalk, making engine noises and weaving in and out of the crowd. Nobody looked at him strangely. Nobody paid any attention to him at all.

After that he often ran into his new friends. Sometimes one of the boys gave him a lift home on the back of his bike. It was great to wheel through the crowds on the busy street, speed down the road by the canal with the wind in his face. Often he didn't get home until after dark. He knew the others would be waiting for their dinner, fidgety and bored, but that wasn't his fault.

Some days the boys just hung around the convenience store. The manager never seemed to mind. Besides, Akira was a good customer. He shopped in that store practically every day. Why shouldn't he hang out there? He started taking his turn buying snacks and games. It was only fair.

One day one of his friends bought a new home video game, but they didn't have anywhere to play it.

"My place," Akira offered. "Our screen's big."

"What about your parents?"

"Not a problem."

His brother and sisters practically leaped out of

their skins when the three boys burst into the apartment.

"You're late," Kyoko said. "How come — "

"I'm here now," Akira announced. "We brought stuff." He pulled out bottles of Coke. He hadn't brought anything for dinner.

The tiny apartment seemed even smaller as the big boys plunked themselves in front of the TV and hooked up the game. Shige ran to join them. Kyoko moved aside to let them pass. Yuki got up from her puzzle and went to stand beside her.

Akira wouldn't look at his sisters.

"Hey! Coke for me!" one of the boys shouted, and Akira turned back to his friends.

Shige plunged into the middle of the group. He wanted a turn, but the boys ignored him.

"Samurai legend!" he cried. "Power of fire!"

"That's not what we're playing, you jerk!"

"Power of fire!"

"Go away, Shige," Akira said.

"Power — !"

"Dammit, shut up, jerk! You're in the way!" One of the boys shoved Shige roughly, pushing him into the wall.

Spring

That did it. Shige crawled to a corner of the room and sat there, his knees pulled up to his chin, quiet and still for once. Akira kept his eyes glued to the television screen.

When the snacks ran out, the boys got restless.

"Let's go back to the store. I'm hungry. Your treat, Akira."

"Sure."

"I want to come, too!" Shige cried.

"No. You stay home. Don't touch the game," Akira said.

"Yeah, kid. Don't touch it." The boys pushed past him and left.

At the store the boys took their time, wandering through the aisles, fingering the boxes of action figures, flipping through the comics, sneaking peeks at the adult magazines.

"Hey, look at her tits," one of them smirked, nudging Akira and pointing to one of the photos. "They're huge! Great, eh?"

Akira didn't really look. He was watching the other boy slip one of the action figures into his pocket.

"What are you doing?" Akira hissed. But the boys

just shoved chips and drinks into his arms and pushed him toward the counter to pay.

The clerk smiled at Akira. It was the nice clerk, the one who had helped him with the New Year's envelopes.

"New friends?" she asked, and he nodded.

Outside the store, the boys pulled him into a dark doorway. They tossed the stolen box at him.

"Here. For you. Now it's your turn."

He just stood there. He didn't know what to say.

"Come on, Akira. It's your turn. Go back to the store." They stared at him hard.

This was a test. He knew it. They were the first real friends he'd ever had.

But he just stood there, and finally the boys got fed up.

"Hey, wait," he said. But they were already on their bikes, wheeling away down the street.

He looked at the toy, still in his hand.

Jetfire. The one he wanted.

How did they know?

HE THOUGHT he would bump into the boys again in the convenience store or at the arcade, but he didn't.

He missed them. Missed having guys to joke around with. Missed passing chips back and forth on their bikes.

So in the end he went to wait for them at their school.

He got there way too early. The school gates were locked, the building quiet.

What would it be like behind those walls, he wondered. Being with other kids, learning stuff, listening to a teacher explain things. Putting up your hand to answer a question, playing ball at recess, wearing a uniform just like all the others—the girls in their tidy skirts and sailor blouses, the boys in their stiff black jackets with the smart rows of brass buttons.

Nobody Knows

What would it be like to go to school?

Finally, the bell rang, the gates magically slid open, and hundreds of kids came pouring out the doors, talking and laughing with each other, their book bags bouncing against their sides.

Then he saw them.

"Hey!" he called out.

"Oh, hey." The boys wandered over with a couple of their friends. "What's up?"

"I bought a new game," Akira said. "Why don't you come over?"

"Maybe when I have time. See you around."

"Got cram school. Sorry." And they headed off with their pals. He could hear their deep boy voices rumbling below the squealing and shrieking of the younger kids.

"Who was that?" he heard one of the boys say. "Can I come, too, when you go over to his place?"

"He's nobody. Besides, his house stinks."

"Stinks of what?"

"Stinks of garbage and stuff. The place is a real pigsty."

"Really? You mean like rotting garbage? No way..."

But by that time their laughter had faded, and Akira could barely tell them apart from the sea of uniforms disappearing down the street.

The school ground cleared so fast, before he had time to think about what to do next. That's when he noticed a small group of girls huddled together, peering around a corner at the bike racks.

"Here she comes!" one of them said, and they ran off giggling.

He wandered over to see what they had been looking at.

It was the girl from the bridge. The girl he had seen on Christmas Eve, throwing her books in the canal. She was alone now, too, staring down at something on the pavement.

Akira went closer. She was looking at some kind of ugly little fake shrine. There were some dead flowers stuffed into a pair of shoes, a stick of incense leaning out of a broken tea cup, a dirty stuffed teddy bear hanging by its neck from a pole, and a handmade cardboard sign.

Nobody Knows

For Saki, it said. *Dead in Heaven*.

This girl must be Saki. He was practically standing right beside her when she turned to look at him.

She had the saddest face he had ever seen.

IT WASN'T LONG after that when the knocking started. The sharp raps on the apartment door that would make all of them stop whatever they were doing and go silent, like they were frozen statues. Then an invisible hand would push an official-looking piece of paper under the door. Papers crowded with tiny print and numbers and words that Akira couldn't understand: *In arrears…account outstanding…no further reminders …service suspended…*

Then the footsteps would go away, echoing down the hallway, and his brother and sisters would turn and look at him, like he was the grownup, like he should know what was happening and how to make it better. Kyoko would stare at him with those black eyes of hers. Shige would turn away from him and go back to the TV. And Yuki would just hang onto his sleeve, her tiny fingers digging into his arm.

He had to do something.

He asked the nice clerk at the convenience store.

"I can help put out the garbage," he told her. "Sweep the floors, stock the shelves…"

"How old are you?" she asked.

"Twelve."

"You can't start working part-time until you're sixteen."

Akira said nothing.

"Shouldn't you…" The clerk went quiet. He knew she was looking at his frayed jacket, his dirty sneakers. He never wore a school uniform, but she seemed to be the only one who noticed.

"Shouldn't you…contact the police?" she asked softly. "Or child welfare or something?"

He shook his head sharply. "I can't. If I do, they'll split us up. We won't be able to stay together. That happened before and it was a big mess. My mother, she couldn't…"

The clerk nodded. They stood silently together for a few minutes, but there was really nothing more to say.

The rain started after that. Week after week of steady drizzle, the clouds low. Even Akira hated going out in that weather. He couldn't buy much anymore anyway. He had spent his baseball-glove money long ago.

He was sitting at the table, counting the money they had left one more time, when a hand thrust a wad of bills in front of him.

"Here," Kyoko said. It was her New Year's money.

"But you need it. For your piano."

"It doesn't matter."

She turned away and sat down on the futon, her chin pressed against her knees. Yuki was sitting on the floor, staring down at her latest drawing, broken bits of crayons scattered around her. Shige lay on his back, pointing his toy ray gun at some invisible enemy on the ceiling.

Akira saw their stringy hair, their thin wrists poking out of too-small clothes, their sagging hems and missing buttons. The blank, bored looks on their faces.

And that's when he decided.

Enough was enough.

THE NEXT morning the sun was shining. Kyoko knew something was different when she saw Akira kneeling beside the closet, pulling out pairs of shoes.

One pair of shoes for each of them.

She smiled, and he looked up at her and grinned.

They waited until the way was clear, and then the four children flew out of the building and into the street. They leaped over the leftover rain puddles. Above them the cherry blossoms were out, the trees green and leafy. The air smelled so good, so clean. A plane soared overhead, flying low, coming from the airport, and Yuki looked up at its silver belly. She smiled as she watched the jet arc across the blue sky.

Their legs were weak and not used to walking, but being outside at last gave them fresh energy. Everything felt new and exciting. The changing traffic lights, the color of the spring grass.

Akira led the way. The others were a bit nervous about all the people on the shopping street, but nobody paid the four kids any attention.

First stop was the store, and they went wild, sliding down the shiny aisles, not sure what to pick first. Noodles, Shige's favorite. Apollo chocolates for Yuki. Akira let the little ones spend their New Year's money on candy and toys. They loaded up their basket with everything they needed.

"Did your mother come back?" The nice clerk at the cash smiled when she saw their basket overflowing.

Akira nodded before the others could answer. But she was already busy scanning their groceries.

The park was next. They had the whole place to themselves. They ran from the swings to the climbing bars to the merry-go-round, spinning and laughing. They breathed in the stink of sunshine. They were drunk on sunshine.

They stopped by a small construction site on the way home, and that's when they all spotted them. Tiny wildflowers growing out of a drainage grate, bright red flowers swaying on long stems.

The little kids were drawn to those flowers like they were rubies. They couldn't dig up the plant, though. Its roots were somewhere deep under the grate. And if they picked the flowers they would soon be dead.

But they couldn't stand to just leave it. Such a brave plant, reaching up through the grate to the sunshine. Its red blossoms seemed to be waving for help in the spring breeze.

"Look, there are seeds," Kyoko said, pushing the petals gently aside.

"Let's take them home," Yuki said.

"Okay, these ones, too. Somebody just left them behind."

"Poor little things."

Soon they had a whole handful.

"We need some dirt, too."

Shige was good at collecting it. He found damp black clods under the rubble and gathered it in one of their plastic shopping bags.

At home they had lots of plastic containers to use as pots. Akira showed them how to make a little shallow hole in the soil with your finger and then drop in

the seed and cover it up very gently. Soon, he said, a flower would be born.

Then they labeled their pots with their names.

"Mine looks funny," Yuki said when she tried to write on the slippery plastic. So Akira put his hand over hers and helped her write her name on her container.

They lined up their pots on the balcony. The sun was setting. They could practically imagine their little plants starting to grow already.

It had been a very good day.

"I'll get water," Kyoko said, turning to go inside.

From inside the apartment her voice sounded echoey.

"The lights aren't working," she called out.

Akira went to check. He pulled the light cord but nothing happened. He unscrewed the bulb and shook it.

"No light in the bathroom, either," Kyoko told him.

His heart dropped.

From the fridge door, Yuki's Mommy picture stared at him, the black crayon eyes round and empty.

SUMMER

As the weather grew warmer things somehow seemed a bit easier, even without electricity, even after the water in their apartment was shut off. They stopped worrying about staying inside. And they found out it was dead easy to come and go without attracting anyone's attention. Nobody seemed to notice four kids living on their own right under their noses. It was as though the children were invisible.

The playground was always empty during the weekdays. There was a bathroom and a public fountain where they could wash themselves and their clothes, too. Shige and Yuki could play on the merry-go-round and swings, and it was nice and shady beneath the trees. They hunted for cicadas and chased the fluffy cottonwood seeds that floated all sparkly in the sun. Yuki called them sun fairies.

Afterwards they would all go home. Akira carried a bucket of fresh water for the apartment. Kyoko carried the laundry. And the little ones would be tired out and ready to sleep as soon as dusk fell.

For a while it was like having their own private kingdom to play in.

Until they noticed the other girl.

It was Saki, the girl Akira had seen at the school. The one the other girls were mean to. The one nobody liked. She sat by herself on a bench at the edge of the park, her book bag at her side. Her school uniform was always clean. Her black school shoes were shiny. She would sit there and thumb her phone and stare at it. She never talked to anyone on it, though.

It was Shige who spoke to her first.

"What are you doing?" he asked.

The girl didn't look up. She looked like a doll, she was so still. Her white sailor blouse was very white.

"Not going to school?"

"No."

"How come?"

"I hate school."

"So why come here?"

She shrugged. "No place else to go."

"Me, neither." He fidgeted and scuffed his sandal into the sand for a moment, but she didn't answer. Then he was off again, exploring behind a nearby tree.

"Hey, did you know there's a cicada hole down here?" he asked, crouching down and grubbing away at the dirt with a stick.

She did look up then, and saw him peeking at her from behind the tree, his smile huge on his round, dirt-smeared face.

She couldn't help smiling back.

It was fun having someone else to play with. Saki played Rock, Paper, Scissors with them and didn't even mind when Yuki shouted out Strawberry instead of Rock, or Airplane instead of Scissors, or when Shige dawdled and they all had to wait for him while he stopped to check every phone booth or vending machine for forgotten coins or candy.

Saki just smiled when he did all that, and that made Akira and Kyoko smile, too.

And she didn't ask a lot of awkward questions. Not

even when she saw the apartment for the first time.

She noticed everything, though. The piles of garbage. The clammy, warm fridge holding nothing but a bottle of water. The sink piled full of dirty dishes. The television in the corner being used as a towel rack. Fruit stickers decorating the doorframes, and what looked like bills taped to the walls and cupboards.

Lots of drawings were simply labeled "Mommy."

She saw the table covered with advertising flyers and stubs of crayons and official-looking notices. *Your rent is overdue. Final Notice Electricity. We have suspended your water service.*

She saw the tangly garden of weeds growing in old soup containers on the balcony.

What could she do? Nothing at all. So she went out to the balcony to help the little ones water their garden.

SAKI CAME OVER lots after that. She drew pictures with Yuki. She and Kyoko made up tinkly duets on the tiny red piano.

The three girls were alone in the apartment the day the door suddenly swung open and there was the landlady clutching her little black-and-white dog.

"Excuse me," she said. "But the door was unlocked." The two older girls looked up. They didn't speak. Yuki had fallen asleep. Her head lay on Saki's lap. Strands of her hair were stuck to her cheeks. She looked very tiny.

"I'm the landlord from the third floor," the woman said. She stepped into the apartment, but she didn't know where to look. Saki had helped them tidy up a bit, but the place was still a mess, a disaster.

"I'm here about the...rent," she went on. "Where is your mother?"

"She's working," Kyoko said after a long pause. "In Osaka."

"Are you cousins, then?" the woman asked. And practically before they could both nod, she was already backing out of the apartment, as if she was afraid to hear or see any more.

It was August, and so hot, even for Tokyo. The days were sweltering and the nights were worse. None of them could breathe in the apartment. It was as if there was no air.

Still, Kyoko and Yuki mostly stayed indoors now, so hungry and tired that they didn't even want to go to the park. So Akira took Shige out with him. It was a nuisance, but Shige went a little crazy these days if he was cooped up too long.

They usually ended up at the convenience store. The nice clerk no longer worked there, but Akira and a new clerk had a routine. Akira would go into the store with an empty blue bucket and pretend to read the comics on the rack. If the clerk made eye contact with him, Akira would go around to the back of the store, and wait. Sometimes he had to wait a long time, but eventually the clerk would come out and slide a couple of packages of day-old sushi into Akira's bucket. Then he would quickly slip back into the store, practically before Akira could say thank you.

Shige was waiting at the front of the store as usual. He was watching a bunch of boys gathered around their shiny bikes, slurping ice creams and complaining about the heat. They ignored Shige, who stared at the icy treats, his face grimy, his filthy T-shirt sticking to his back.

Akira had to call him twice before he tore his eyes away from the boys and trotted down the street after his brother.

"Is there salmon?" Shige asked, trying to peer into the bucket.

"No. Just what's here."

"No fair."

ON THE DAYS when Saki came over, Akira would walk her home. Kyoko watched them. She'd noticed that on those days her brother would wash his hair at the park, sniff his clothes to find a T-shirt that didn't smell too bad. She'd noticed that his voice sounded weird sometimes, like he was catching a cold or something.

Akira and Saki always took their time getting to her place. It was as though neither of them was in a hurry to go home.

One hot muggy day, Saki stopped beside a vending machine and bought two sodas. The expensive kind that came in the blue aluminum bottles.

"Nice and cool?" she said, pressing one gently against Akira's cheek.

He smiled. It was a treat to have a soda from the machine. And it was nice and cold.

Summer

Saki lived in a small tidy building with a gate that locked. Trim green bushes lined the walkway that led to the front entrance. She never invited him in. He didn't expect her to.

"When is your mother coming home?" she asked suddenly, as she turned to say goodbye.

"She isn't," Akira said. "She's never coming back."

Saki stopped and looked at him, a hundred questions in her eyes.

"Probably," he said gruffly. "She's probably never coming back."

Later that night he sat up, fingering the bright blue cap from the drink Saki had bought for him. He polished it with his shirt. He liked the way it gleamed in the glow of the streetlight.

The apartment was so hot and stuffy, but his sisters and brother were asleep all around him. They looked like worn-out puppies, their arms and legs tangled in the sheets.

Akira stared at them for a long time.

Their mother was never coming back.

Probably never coming back.

"I CAN MAKE some money," Saki said the next day. Akira was walking her home as usual.

"What?" he said. "How?"

She turned to him and grinned. Then she got out her phone and started punching numbers.

They went to the train station. He watched her from the other side of the street while she waited by the entrance.

Soon a man came up the stairs. He went over to Saki and they greeted each other. Akira didn't think Saki knew the man, though he stood with his head close to hers as they talked. He was wearing a black business suit and carrying a briefcase. He was short, with not much hair. He was old.

Saki and the man walked back into the station.

Akira waited. And the longer he waited, the worse he felt.

She was gone for a long time, and it was dark when she finally came back with the man. They turned to each other and said goodbye, and he left.

Saki came flying across the street to Akira. She thrust out her hand at him. It was full of tightly folded bills.

"Here!" she said.

Akira looked at the money. Then he looked up at her. He felt sick.

"No."

"Why not? I just sang karaoke with him."

Akira stared at her, at her hand, still stretched out. She was lying.

"No!" he yelled, and he turned and ran.

He ran for a long time, past the bright storefronts. His sandals slapped hard on the pavement. He ran until he felt like throwing up, but when he finally stopped, his stomach heaving, he couldn't even do that.

THE NEXT MORNING Akira woke up hot and sweaty. The sheets smelled. It had been a long time since they had aired out the bedding. The balcony was crowded with all their plastic pots full of dying plants and spilled dirt, and no one had the energy to clean it up.

The girls were still sleeping, but he could hear the sound of chewing.

It was Shige, and he had something in his mouth.

"What are you eating?" Akira said quietly. "Spit it out."

He held out his hand. Shige sat up and leaned over and spat a white lump into his brother's palm.

"What is that?"

Shige lay back down and rolled over, turning his back to his brother.

"Paper," he whispered. "I was eating paper."

Akira made his way down the hill slowly, a large container of noodles balanced in each hand. The clerk had given them to him for free because the seals were broken, but he had to carry them carefully or they would spill.

Still, Shige would be happy. He loved noodles.

But when he arrived back in the apartment, only Yuki was there. She didn't get up to greet him — she never did anymore — but just turned slowly to face him.

"Where's Shige?" Akira said, placing the noodles on the table.

"Don't know." Yuki's voice was very small. She looked pale and skinny, her eyes like deep black pools.

"What about Kyoko?" he said.

Yuki looked over at the closed closet door.

Akira whipped it open. Kyoko was sitting on the floor of the closet in the dark, her face buried in the flowered blouse their mother had worn the night she brought home the sushi. Her last night at home, really.

His sister had been crying, he could tell, but he had no time for that right now.

"What are you doing?" he shouted. "Where's Shige?"

"I don't know. He left. He said he was hungry."

Akira ran from the apartment. Didn't the kid know the damn rules? Hadn't their mother made it clear?

He was furious. Furious at Shige. Furious at them all when he was trying so hard to keep it together.

It wasn't his fault!

He ran and ran, and he finally found his brother playing with some kids who had a bunch of robot cars. Akira had to scream to get his attention.

"You said you wanted noodles, so I got some!"

Shige barely looked up. His hands were on the remote control. He was concentrating, trying to make his truck move behind...

"What do you want?" he muttered.

Summer

Akira was so mad, so mad at all of them.

"Do what you want!" he yelled. "And don't bother coming home!" He kicked Shige's truck into the wall, where it bounced once and landed on the sidewalk.

Shige stared at his brother.

"Don't be mad at the truck!" he shouted, while his new friends rushed to see whether the battery was still working. "It's just my brother," he told them. "He's an idiot."

But as Akira stomped his way back home, he turned and saw Shige trotting after him.

It was little Yuki who finally made him crazy. They were all just lying around the apartment, the smells of their garbage, of their own unwashed bodies filling the room in the heat. They mostly just slept now. No energy to go out, to wash, even to talk.

Yet here was Yuki plunking on that stupid toy piano. She didn't know any tunes, but she kept slamming down those tinny keys until he couldn't stand it anymore.

"Cut it out, Yuki!" he screamed.

She stared at him, like she didn't even know who he was.

"I have to go pee," she said, her voice tiny.

"Why didn't you pee in the park before?"

Didn't she know there was no water? That the toilet didn't flush?

She just stared at him. She was only five. He shouldn't be mean to her but somehow knowing this made him madder than ever.

"Go pee in the bathtub."

"I don't want to." She was quiet for a moment. "When is Saki coming back?"

Akira couldn't stand to look at her sad face for another second, full of questions he couldn't answer. Her eyes began to fill up, even though she never cried.

He got up and went to the refrigerator. The inside smelled of plastic. Why even use it when there was no electricity?

He reached for the water bottle, but it was gone.

"Shige!" His brother was out on the balcony, the precious water bottle in his fat little hands as he tried to water their sad excuse for a garden. When he accidentally knocked one of his own plants off the railing and it tumbled to the ground below, Akira almost felt like cheering.

"Shigeru!" he yelled. "You can't just use up all the water! There's nothing left to drink!"

"Is Saki coming over to play again?" Yuki asked.

"No. Never again." He was really mad now. How could his mother do this to him? What was he supposed to do? He was twelve years old. It wasn't his fault.

He yanked open the closet door. All his mother's clothes hung there. Her party dresses, her scarves. She loved pretty things.

It made him crazy to see her clothes there. He began to yank them off the hangers, throw them to the floor.

"What are you doing?" Kyoko cried.

"I'm selling these. We don't need them anymore."

"Don't! Stop it!" She grabbed the blouse with the flowers and tried to pull it out of his hands.

"Cut it out. Let go!" They'd never had a fight before. Not like this.

"Shut up!"

"Get out of the way!" He glared at her, at her thin, thin face.

But he had to say it anyway.

"Don't you get it? She's not coming back! She's never coming back!"

And then he couldn't stand it anymore. He let go of the blouse, threw it back in his sister's face.

"Stay in the closet then, you idiot! Who cares!"

He looked around the apartment. At the garbage, the mess. At all those stupid drawings Yuki had made. The filthy sheets and quilts that they couldn't wash anymore because there was no water. At the dying plants on the balcony leaking their mud all over the floor. At Shige's dirty feet, Kyoko clutching their mother's blouse with the white flowers on it. At Yuki's big, big eyes just staring at him.

He had never shouted at his sister like this before.

And he turned and ran out of the apartment.

IT TOOK HIM a long time to calm down. Eventually his feet took him to the schoolyard.

He stood outside the chainlink fence, feeling like a prisoner even though he was on the outside looking in. He realized it must be a Saturday. Boys his age were getting ready for a baseball game, warming up on the field, looking so smart in their matching caps, shirts, socks and shoes.

A few parents sat in the stands. They held umbrellas to shield them from the hot sun. They waved fans at their faces. They had bottles of cold water at their sides.

The White Bears were playing the Kenzan Fighters.

The White Bears coach was watching his players practicing on one side of the field. Some kids were fielding ground balls, some were batting.

"Miyauchi!" he shouted. "You're moving your legs too much!" He consulted his clipboard.

"Kato! Where's Yano today?"

"Cram school," a boy shouted.

"Cram school?" The coach flung down his clipboard and scratched his head. "That means we're short."

He scanned the field and his eyes came to rest on Akira, sitting outside the fence. The coach narrowed his eyes and grinned. Then he headed Akira's way.

The uniform was way too big on Akira's skinny shoulders, but he didn't care. Number nine, that was his number. The socks fit, and the shoes fit perfectly!

And the glove. The glove was real leather, soft and shiny and golden brown. Coach showed him how to put his index finger in the thumb part, how to let the ball sink into the soft pouch, how to close the glove on the ball so he wouldn't lose it.

The two teams met in the center of the field and bowed. Then the umpire blew his whistle, and Coach sent Akira out to play right field.

The other boys didn't seem to care that he was new. They didn't have enough players, and without him there would be no game.

It was pretty quiet out in right field, but Akira didn't mind. He kept his eye on the game, watching every play, crouched over and bouncing on his toes the way he'd seen the others do, just in case the ball came his way.

Nothing happened for a long time...

And then it did. The ball came flying toward him. He held up his arm but the ball went sailing past. He ran for it as it skidded off the wall at the end of the field. He chased after it, scooped it up. And when he turned there was one of his teammates ready to receive the throw, just the way the pros did on TV.

He was playing. He was really doing it. His face split into a huge grin, and he laughed.

At the end of the inning he was nervous about going up to bat.

His first swing was stiff, too late.

Coach trotted to the plate and stood behind him.

"Akira, hold your hands together, like this." He moved Akira's hands closer together and placed his own hands over them to show him how to grip the bat. "Keep your eye on the ball, and when it comes, take a real hard slice at it. Wham. Just wham, swing away."

Akira nodded. He could do it. No one had ever shown him how before.

The second pitch came and Akira swung away. He missed again, but Coach's voice came from the side-lines.

"That's a nice swing, Akira. A fine swing."

His teammates were cheering him on, too. They called his name. "Let's go!" "Come on, Akira!"

It gave him courage, and with the next pitch the ball and the bat connected.

He almost forgot to run at first, but then he did and he made it to first base with the cheers of his teammates ringing in his ears.

It was the best feeling he'd ever had.

It was the greatest day of his life.

THE CHEERS OF the crowd were still echoing in Akira's head as he ran home. He could still feel the end of the bat snug in his hands, still hear the crack when he made contact with the ball. He remembered the feeling of his feet slipping into real sports sneakers. And they'd fit him! He hadn't hit or caught the ball every time, but he'd played, just like the others.

He wished his brother and sisters could have been there, cheering on the sidelines, watching him play with the other kids, part of the team.

His team. The White Bears.

He took the stairs two at a time and ran down the hall. They'd be extra mad at him for being late, but so what? He'd make it up to Shige. Get him more of his favorite noodles, somehow.

He opened the door. And saw everything at once.

Summer

The flimsy yellow folding chair, tipped on its side by the window. Kyoko hugging her knees, rocking back and forth. Shige huddled in a corner, his cheek pressed against the wall.

And between them lay Yuki, crumpled up on the floor.

"Yuki?" he called.

Kyoko lifted her face to him.

"She was trying to reach the cups," she whispered. "She fell off the chair. She won't get up."

"Yuki!" He ran to her and bent down, shook her. Gently at first, then harder.

Her small body was completely still.

Akira stumbled through the crowded street, past the brightly lit stores. The faces of the crowd were a blur, the lights were blinding him.

For the first time in his life, he had no idea what to do. So many stores, but no place he could go. So many people, but nobody he could tell.

Almost nobody.

He waited outside Saki's house until she got home. She saw his face, and she knew the news was bad.

"Akira, what happened?"

"That money that you...can I borrow it?" He didn't know how to say it. "I want it to show Yuki...the airplanes."

They stopped at the convenience store on the way back to the apartment, gathering up every single box of Apollo chocolates on the shelf and piling them neatly on the counter.

"Are you going on a picnic or something?" the clerk said. "Looks like fun."

Back at the apartment the others were waiting. There was a strange envelope on the table.

"Kyoko? What's this?" Akira asked.

"It just came."

He opened it up. The wad of bank notes was thick. The accompanying note was very short:

To Akira
Give them my best. I'm counting on you.
Mother

NIGHT CAME. They lit a candle. It made a little circle of light as they gathered to take care of Yuki.

They tried the brown suitcase first. It seemed like a good choice, the one she had come in. They were very gentle with her. But the suitcase was too small.

"She doesn't fit," Akira said.

"I guess…she grew." Kyoko fetched the big pink suitcase—Shige's case. Yuki fit easily in that one.

They made sure she had everything she needed. Kyoko found Yuki's favorite red slippers, the ones with the brown bears. The shoes squeaked a bit as she slipped them on Yuki's feet. They tucked her bunny inside her small, cool fist. Then they placed the boxes of Apollos all around her like flowers and closed the lid.

Akira and Saki carried the case down the stairs

carefully. From the balcony, Kyoko and Shige watched the two older children ease the case onto the sidewalk.

"Is this goodbye?" Shige asked, looking up at Kyoko.

She didn't answer. Just reached for his hand and held it tight as they watched Akira and Saki roll the suitcase slowly down the street toward the rush-hour crowds and the monorail.

It was late by the time they came to the field near the airport. The ground trembled and the air was filled with the shriek of the jets taking off and landing. Their lights swept the ground like spotlights. For a moment Akira and Saki just sat watching the planes come and go. The breeze was cool here, away from all the concrete of the city.

The ground was soft, and they took turns breaking it up with a piece of wood they found nearby. After that they dug with their hands, on their knees and hunched over, like they were making a sand castle at the beach.

In the end the hole was quite shallow, but it still took a long time.

They laid the suitcase in gently and stared at it together for a moment. They didn't say anything. Then

Summer

Akira cupped his hands full of earth and threw it on the case. He rested his empty hands on his knees, his muddy fingers trembling.

Saki placed her hand on his fingers to quiet them. He couldn't cry, so she wept silently for them both.

Dawn was breaking by the time they were finished. They sat side by side on the train as the monorail took them back to the city. The sky and the calm waters of the bay looked mauve in the morning light, and the city was gleaming, clean and bright in the rising sun.

AKIRA SAT ON the pavement outside the back door of the convenience store and waited in his regular spot. Before long the clerk came out and silently dumped a pile of day-old sushi into the bucket.

Kyoko, Saki and Shige were waiting out front. The air was thick with heat as the four children made their way through the crowd. The faces of the passing shoppers were blank, their steps slow. Nobody gave the children a second glance. Saki and Kyoko walked ahead a bit, talking quietly together, their arms sometimes touching.

At the crosswalk they all stopped to wait for the traffic to pass, and through the sounds of the crowd and the cars, Akira heard a distant drone.

He looked up. High in the sky was a plane, coming from the direction of the airport, still climbing, the sun glinting off its gleaming body like a beacon.

Summer

He watched it soar, disappearing like a silver bird into the blue, higher and higher...

Until he felt a gentle tug on his sleeve. It was Shige, gazing up at his brother, his round face puzzled.

Akira stood taller. The traffic had cleared, and the others were waiting on the other side. Time to cross.

The streets gradually grew quieter as the four children headed back to the apartment. Shige lagged behind as usual, muttering to himself in time to some soundless drum inside his head.

At the corner he ran up to the vending machine, running his hand through the trough, crouching down to reach for a jammed chocolate bar, a forgotten coin. But there was nothing.

He checked the pay phone next, reaching up to pull open the coin collector.

"Found one!" he cried suddenly. He raised his fist in triumph and ran to join the others.

The children turned to look at him. At his joyful, sweat-streaked face, at the silver coin in his grubby hand.

And they all smiled, before they turned and continued on their way.